W9-AMU-356

Bring Back Barkley

Marilyn D. Anderson

illustrated by Mel Crawford

To Harry Boling,
whose years of hard work have
given me time to write books

PAGES
Publishing Group ™

First printing by Willowisp Press 1998.

Published by Willowisp Press
801 94th Avenue North, St. Petersburg, Florida 33702

Copyright © 1998 by PAGES Publishing Group. All rights reserved.
No portion of this book may be reproduced, stored in a retrieval system,
or transmitted, in any form or by any means, electronic, mechanical,
photocopying, recording, or otherwise, without written
permission from the publisher.

Printed in the United States of America

Willowisp Press®

2 4 6 8 10 9 7 5 3 1

ISBN 0-87406-890-8

One

"**R**uff! Ruff!" barked Barkley Boggs. The whiskery-faced dog looked up at his boy Jamie. It was a Sunday afternoon in late October, and they were at Mrs. Williams's house. Mrs. Williams and Barkley were best friends.

Barkley looked at the two strange men who had just walked into the room carrying Mrs. Williams's sofa. What was going on here? Why were they taking Mrs. Williams's couch? Wasn't anyone going to stop them?

"Ruff! Ruff!" Barkley barked again.

"Barkley!" Jamie Boggs said firmly. "Leave them alone. They're supposed to do that. Mrs.

Williams is moving out today and we're here to tell her goodbye, remember?"

Barkley lowered his ears and lay flat on the floor. He wasn't sure exactly what Jamie had said, but he knew that he had just been scolded.

Tim, Mrs. Williams's son, held the door for the men. The first man backed out the door carrying one end of the sofa. The second man followed holding the other end.

"'Bye, Mrs. Williams," the man said as he carried out the sofa. "I know you'll love Sunny Acres."

"Thank you, Fred," she called out, waving from her wheelchair. "And thanks for helping me with the move."

Barkley looked around the room. The whole place was empty. He walked from corner to corner, sniffing the air. His claws made clicking sounds on the wooden floors.

Then he spotted a small piece of newspaper on the floor. He flopped down next to it. He began to chew it half-heartedly.

"Barkley, no!" ordered Jamie, and he pulled the paper out of Barkley's mouth.

Barkley whined. Ever since they'd moved to Indiana, it seemed Jamie was always scolding him. And to make matters worse, Jamie took him to 4-H obedience class every week now. Barkley hated that.

Barkley got up and walked over to Mrs. Williams. He put his head in her lap so she could pet him. Mrs. Williams stroked Barkley's ears with her soft hands. "Oh, Barkley, Love," she said softly. "I know I need to make the move to Sunny Acres, but I'm going to miss you. After all, you saved my life!"

When the Boggs family had first moved to Indiana, Barkley had found his way out of the garage and visited Mrs. Williams every day.

One day Barkley had discovered Mrs. Williams lying very still inside her kitchen. He had brought help. Mrs. Williams had gone to the hospital for a while. Then, when she came home, Mr. Boggs had brought Barkley to see her every morning. The two spent their days together. Jamie would come to pick him up when school was over. Sometimes Jamie's friend, Melissa, would come over, too. Those had been happy times for Barkley.

But lately Mrs. Williams had been having some dizzy spells. Now it seemed that she was leaving the house for some reason.

"Oh, Mom," said Tim, coming over to put his arm around Mrs. Williams. "If you'd only move to Texas, you could live with Lisa and me."

Mrs. Williams smiled and nodded. She stroked Barkley's ears a little harder. "I know," she said. "But Indiana is my home, and all of my friends are at Sunny Acres now. It probably will be nice living there. It's just that it will be a bit different, that's all."

"You'll be too busy to notice the difference," Tim said, patting her arm. "Sunny Acres has quite a schedule of activities—card parties, exercise classes, and even a bird-watching group."

Mrs. Williams sighed. "It's not Sunny Acres I'm worried about. It really is a lovely place. It's just that I've heard some rumors about their new manager. Mr. Peach is his name. Some of my friends don't like him very much."

"I've met him and he seems nice enough," Tim answered.

"I suppose I'll get used to him," Mrs. Williams said. "Still, I'm going to miss Barkley. And he's going to miss my cookies." She wheeled toward the cookie jar on the counter. She pulled the jar slowly down into her lap and took out a cookie. She held it up to Barkley.

"Barkley, here's an oatmeal cookie," she said sweetly.

Barkley hadn't understood everything else that had been said, but he knew about cookies. He scrambled over to Mrs. Williams and sat for her. He tipped his head to one side so that one ear stood up. Then he raised his left paw and said, "Ruff!"

Mrs. Williams grinned. "Good dog," she said, handing Barkley the cookie. He gobbled it down. It was delicious.

"You'll like bird watching," said Jamie. "My dad has a bird feeder right outside our kitchen window, and even Barkley likes to watch the birds come. But you should hear him bark at the squirrels! They eat the bird food and keep the birds away."

Mrs. Williams petted Barkley's head some more.

"Well, Barkley's a smart one," she said.

She looked at the ceiling and sighed. "I know it's for the best, but I do hate the thought of leaving this old house."

"Lisa and I will come up for Christmas," Tim promised. "And by then you'll have your own apartment—with all of your own things. Even that old couch."

"Yes, that will be nice," she said. "But I won't have Barkley."

"Well, I'll bring Barkley to Sunny Acres tomorrow," said Jamie.

Barkley's ears went up at the mention of his name.

Mrs. Williams turned to Jamie. "Oh, that would be lovely," she said, brightening. "Do you suppose Sunny Acres will allow it?"

"Sure," said Jamie. "Why wouldn't they?"

Just then Barkley heard a car drive up. He ran to the door and wagged his tail.

"Oh, that's probably Dad," said Jamie. Sure enough, a knock sounded at the door and Jamie's dad came in.

"Hello, Mrs. Williams. Hello, Tim," he said, shaking hands with Tim. "Did you all have a nice visit?"

"Lovely," said Mrs. Williams, smiling.

"I wish I could stay for a while," said Mr. Boggs," but I've got a meeting at church tonight, so I need to run." He looked at Jamie. "Ready?"

"Ready," Jamie agreed. "Well, goodbye, Mrs. Williams. I'll see you tomorrow."

"Goodbye, Jamie," she answered, giving the boy a small hug. Then she threw her arms wide open for Barkley.

Barkley knew something important was going

on, so he jumped onto Mrs. Williams's lap and licked her face.

"Goodbye, Barkley," she said, sniffling. "Please do come visit me."

Mrs. Williams's voice sounded so sad. On the way out to the car, Barkley whimpered.

Two

The next morning was warm and sunny. Barkley raced out the door to make his rounds. He could hardly wait for Mr. Boggs to drop him off at Mrs. Williams's house. But first he had to do something about some pesky squirrels.

Sure enough, two bushy-tailed robbers were up on the bird feeder stealing seeds. A third was under the feeder grabbing what the other two threw down.

"Ruff, ruff, ruff, ruff!" Barkley barked, launching himself at the squirrel under the feeder.

The squirrel zoomed up the nearest tree.

But the other two just looked down and chattered away at Barkley. He barked and barked, leaping high in the air, but he couldn't reach the squirrels.

Disgusted, Barkley set off to check the rest of the yard. Maybe the sheep were in the pasture out back. He went around behind the garage to see. No, there were no sheep on the other side of the barbed wire today. And Barkley wasn't going into *that* pasture.

A while back, Barkley had gotten in trouble with the man who owned the land—and with the man's nasty German shepherd, Sarge. He didn't want it to happen again!

Suddenly, Barkley heard a strange whistle. It was a sad sound, almost like a person in trouble would make. The sound was coming from the small oak tree just over his head. Barkley looked up.

Suddenly something hit him in the face. It was only a small twig, but it surprised him.

"Ruff?" Barkley barked softly.

Then he saw the mysterious whistler. It was a bird with a very long tail. It looked like a pigeon. But this bird was different. It had a strange bunch of feathers sticking up from its light-colored head.

Its feathers were all fluffed out, and it sat hunched over. It reminded Barkley of the way Mrs. Williams had sat yesterday. Was this bird sad, too? Barkley decided that maybe the bird was hungry. He wanted to show it the bird feeder. Barkley made a high-pitched whine, something like the bird's whistle.

Then he backed away.

The bird turned its head to the side, one beady black eye following Barkley. The bird whistled again and flew to a tree closer to Barkley. Barkley backed up some more, and the bird followed.

Soon they were at the bird feeder. The bird landed on the edge of the platform. It took a sunflower seed in its beak. Then it twisted its beak around the seed. Spitting out the shell, the bird swallowed the inside of the seed. It looked over the edge at Barkley and as if to say "thank you." Then it grabbed another seed.

One of the squirrels, its tail quivering, chattered at the bird. The bird squawked angrily. The squirrel quickly dropped over the side of the platform and ran down the pole. His squirrel friend went down the other side.

"Ruff, ruff!" Barkley barked joyously. Now he could chase those squirrels back where they belonged.

When the squirrels were back in their own tree, Barkley returned to the bird feeder. He watched the new bird hungrily eating more seeds.

"Barkley, come," Barkley heard Jamie call. "I've got to go to school, and you have to go in your pen." The boy came around the corner of the house.

"Barkley, let's—" Jamie stopped and stared at the feeder. "Gosh," he said, "what kind of bird is that?"

"Jamie!" Mrs. Boggs called. "The bus will be here any minute."

"Mom, there's a really weird bird out here," he said.

"That's nice, dear," she said. "But you don't want to miss the bus."

"All right," he called back. He grabbed Barkley's collar and tugged the dog toward the new pen Jamie and his father had made.

"In you go," said the boy. "I hope you like your new kennel."

Barkley did not like the new kennel. Sure, he had food and water and a nice house with a red rug inside. But he was supposed to go to Mrs. Williams's house, not be locked up all day.

"Ruff?" barked Barkley. Jamie went toward the house and disappeared inside.

Barkley sent up a long howl and waited. Nothing happened. He howled again. Still nothing. He went to the gate and tried his teeth on it. The metal hurt his mouth. He tried to dig down with his toes. The ground was too hard.

17

Finally he dropped into a heap. It was going to be a boring day.

"Wheet!" said someone.

Barkley looked up to see the strange bird perched on the upper rim of his kennel.

"Pretty bird," said the visitor.

Barkley's ears shot up. A bird that could talk like a human?

"Pretty bird," the stranger repeated.

Yes, this bird could definitely talk when it wanted to. Flipping around, it hung by its beak from the top rail. Then it swung underneath and returned to a sitting position again.

Barkley was fascinated. He moved closer to the bird, but it flew off. When Barkley backed up again, the bird returned to the rim.

Barkley decided the bird was thirsty but that he was afraid to come down to Barkley's water dish. So Barkley turned and went to the far end of his kennel. He kept his back to the bird, but he peeked over his shoulder to see what would happen next.

The bird hesitated. Then it climbed backward down the fence until it neared the bottom. From there it hopped to the floor of the pen and dipped its beak quickly in the water dish. It eyed Barkley again. Then it dipped back into the water. It dipped again and again. Barkley turned and crept forward a few inches to see better. The bird panicked and fluttered over to the fence. Barkley yawned and rolled over on his back to show he was harmless.

"Smart bird," the newcomer said, and it returned to the water. It jumped in and began to splash. Barkley was so surprised that he sat up and gave a short bark. That sent the bird off in a flurry of feathers toward the garage.

Barkley ran to the fence and leaped into the air. He wanted to fly away, too. He wanted to fly to wherever Mrs. Williams had gone.

Three

When Mrs. Boggs drove in that afternoon, Barkley jumped around joyously.

"Sorry, Barkley," she said. "You'll have to wait for Jamie. He'll be home soon." She went into the house. Barkley groaned and flopped down again to wait. The new bird's visit had been the only interesting part of his day. He wanted action!

Finally the big, yellow bus drove up. Jamie jumped out and ran toward the kennel.

"Hi, Barkley!" he called. "Do you want out of there?"

"Ruff! Ruff! RUFF!" barked Barkley. He whirled around and jumped up and down.

Then Jamie opened the gate, and he and Barkley wrestled with each other. Barkley managed to get on top and lick his boy's nose.

"Hey, cut it out!" said Jamie, laughing, hiding his face, and pushing Barkley away. "I'm ready for a cookie. How about you?"

Barkley sprang to his feet and raced toward the house.

Jamie caught up with Barkley at the door and led him to the cookie jar. He grabbed a cookie for himself and flipped a dog biscuit at Barkley. To Barkley, a biscuit was almost as good as a cookie.

Then Jamie went over to his mother, who was working on some papers at the kitchen table.

"Hey, Mom," he said. "Can you take me to visit Mrs. Williams like we talked about?"

"All right," she answered. "I have to run these papers in to the office anyway. I'll drop you off."

"Race you to the car!" Jamie yelled to Barkley.

*   *   *   *   *

When they arrived at Sunny Acres, Jamie took Barkley to the front desk. A large, gray-haired woman smiled at him from behind a beautiful bouquet of fresh flowers.

"Hi," said the boy. "My name is Jamie, and this is Barkley. We'd like to see Mrs. Myrtle Williams."

"I'm Miss Case. Welcome to Sunny Acres." The woman reached down and petted Barkley. "I think Mrs. Williams is in the lounge. Let's find her."

She led the way down a long hall with bookshelves on either side. Barkley and Jamie followed. Barkley kept sniffing the air. It smelled a little weird—kind of like flowers and soap all mixed together. Gentle music played in the background.

As they walked, they passed a nice, dark-haired lady in a wheelchair. A friendly man was walking along with the help of a metal con-traption. Miss Case called it a walker. Some people sat in the big, cozy armchairs that lined the hall. In fact, the hallway looked like someone's comfortable living room.

Everyone seemed happy to see Barkley. Each person smiled as the dog passed by. Every once in a while, someone reached out and scratched Barkley's head.

"How are you doing, boy?" one plump woman asked.

All the official people who worked at Sunny Acres—those who wore white or light blue and who had official "Sunny Acres" name tags—smiled at Barkley, too.

Finally they got to a room that was almost as big as the room where Barkley went for dog training. Lots of people were sitting around small tables. One young woman in a bright blue shirt stood to one side with her hand in a plastic bucket.

"B-6," said the younger woman.

When she said that, everyone looked down at his or her table. The people seemed to be studying the small cards that were in front of them.

Suddenly, Barkley spotted Mrs. Williams. She was at a table with two other women. He barked twice and then pulled Jamie toward her.

Mrs. Williams gave a little jerk and looked down. Then she smiled a huge smile.

"Barkley!" she cried, reaching for him. Barkley stood on his hind legs to touch her face with his nose.

"Oh, my little Love. You did come to see me," she cooed. "And, Jamie, this is so nice of you."

A lady in a lavender warm-up suit at the next table looked over. "Oh!" she cried. "What a cute dog! May I pet him?"

"Sure," said Jamie.

But before the woman could get to Barkley, another woman with bright red hair wheeled up in her chair.

"Oh, a dog!" she cried. "Oh, I love dogs!"

Three more women and a man left their

tables and soon Barkley and Jamie were surrounded. Barkley pulled his lips back into a grin and wiggled. He loved the attention.

"N-6," the lady in the bright blue called. Only a few people were looking at their cards now.

Then Barkley heard a roar. He knew that sound—it meant that someone was angry! The people around Barkley scattered.

"Arrrgh!" bellowed a tall man in blue jeans and a white shirt. Swinging his cane, he headed right toward Barkley.

"Look out!" cried the red-haired woman. "It's Mr. Hale, and he's out of control again."

Barkley figured that if he could get the man to chase him, the man would leave Mrs. Williams alone. So Barkley wriggled out of her arms and ran. He barked at the old man and zipped by just out of reach of his cane.

Everyone screamed. Someone shouted, "Stop him!"

Barkley ran. He ran fast. While he ran, he

knocked over a table. Cards and tiny things that looked like buttons spilled every which way.

"Barkley, come back!" Jamie wailed.

Then a shrill whistle cut through the noise. Barkley stopped running and looked toward the whistle. He saw in the doorway a short, bald-headed man wearing thick glasses.

"What is the meaning of this?" the man shouted. "Who let that dog in here?"

Barkley felt someone grab his leash. It was Miss Case. Then she reached down and picked him up. He felt her heart beating almost as fast as his was. Was he in trouble again?

Four

At first, no one answered the man, but then the red-haired woman threw her head back and laughed. "Wasn't that fun? I love a little excitement, don't you, Mr. Peach?"

Mr. Peach glared at her. "No!" he snarled. "And I repeat—who let that dog in here?"

"W-w-well, I did," Miss Case said, stuttering. "I didn't see any harm in it."

"No harm?" Mr. Peach said scornfully. "Look at this place. It's a disaster area."

"It's not that bad," said the lady in the lavender warm-up suit.

"And you can't blame the dog," said another man.

"No, it was Jack Hale," said the red-haired woman. "You know how he is about surprises."

"I don't care whose fault you think it was," Mr. Peach said, his voice getting louder. "Just get him out of here or else! I won't have animals in my hospital."

When he pointed at Miss Case and Barkley, Jamie hurried over and took Barkley's leash in his hand.

"This isn't a hospital," the red-haired woman said. "It's our home."

"Yes, yes, Mrs. Swenson," said Mr. Peach. "But dogs carry germs. And we can't have germs around here." His gaze shifted to Jamie. "Young man, you brought this dog in. Now get him out."

"Yes, sir," said Jamie.

As he led Barkley toward the door, the dog hung back. He looked over his shoulder for Mrs. Williams, but she was gone.

"What a nasty guy," Jamie muttered.

"P-s-s-s-t," said someone right behind them.

Barkley looked around to see Miss Case. "Come with me," she whispered.

Jamie and Barkley followed Miss Case into a room with lots of big metal boxes. Towels were everywhere. And the whole room smelled like soap.

"Wait here," she said, whispering. "I'll bring Mrs. Williams."

Minutes later Miss Case returned pushing Mrs. Williams's wheelchair in front of her. Mrs. Williams beamed when she saw Barkley. Barkley jumped up on her knees, and his old friend hugged him long and hard. Then she turned to Jamie and hugged him hard, too. Miss Case grinned and stepped out, closing the door behind her.

"I'm so sorry about all this ruckus," said Mrs. Williams. "Folks say Mr. Peach is new around here, so he thinks he has to prove he's in charge. He wants everything by the book, you know."

"Maybe so," said Jamie. "I just hope Miss

Case doesn't get into trouble over all this."

"Yes," Mrs. Williams agreed. "She's one of my favorite people at Sunny Acres. Now tell me, what's new since yesterday?"

Jamie thought hard. "Well, nothing much," he began. Then he smiled. "Oh, yeah, I saw a really weird bird at the feeder."

"What did it look like?" asked Mrs. Williams.

"It had a yellow head with an orange circle below each eye. And there were a bunch of feathers sticking straight up on its head." He put the heel of his hand sideways on his head with the fingers sticking up.

"Hmmm," said Mrs. Williams. "What color was its body?"

"Mostly gray," said Jamie.

Mrs. Williams frowned. "I've never heard of a bird like that. I'll ask Mrs. Swenson about it— you know, the woman with the red hair. She's our resident bird watcher."

Just then the door opened and Miss Case burst in. "Hide the dog and let's get out of here," she gasped. "Peach is on his way to check out the laundry."

Barkley understood the fear in her voice and looked around wildly. He expected either the man with the cane or the one with the whistle to appear at any moment. He had to hide—and quick!

But before Barkley could run, Mrs. Williams grabbed him and tucked him into her large sweater.

"Let's go," she said, heading for the door. "I don't think Peach should find me here, either."

"Right!" said Miss Case, reaching for the door. "I'll see if the coast is clear." She looked out and nodded.

Barkley was shaking as they wheeled down the hall. He figured that Jamie was probably scared, too. He wished he could see where they were going.

Everything was quiet at first. Then, suddenly, he heard a familiar voice.

"Hold it right there!" shouted Mr. Peach.

"Miss Case, Mrs. Williams, I want to see you in my office right now."

Barkley knew they were in trouble—big trouble.

Five

Barkley held very still and wondered what would happen next. He couldn't see anything from where he was—tucked inside of the waist of Mrs. Williams's sweater.

"Yes, Mr. Peach," said Miss Case, and Barkley heard her walk off.

Mrs. Williams turned her chair around and said, "I'll be there as soon as I give something to Mrs. Swenson."

The chair began to move again. Barkley wanted to see where they were going, so he wriggled to get out of the sweater. A hand pushed him back inside.

"No," whispered Jamie.

"Oh, that Peach!" Mrs. Williams muttered. "I wish he'd leave."

When the chair stopped, Barkley felt the sweater being pulled back a few inches. He found himself looking up at the red-haired woman seated in a wheelchair.

"Oh," said Mrs. Swenson, her eyes widening.

She pulled Barkley toward her lap. Barkley stiffened his legs to object, but the old lady was strong. She shoved him roughly into her lap and dropped a bumpy woolen blanket over his head.

Mrs. Swenson took off quickly. "Got to get you out the door," she whispered. "It's right down here and . . ."

"Mrs. Swenson," a cheerful voice called after them. "Where are you going, dear? It's time for your bath."

The wheelchair stopped.

"Rats!" muttered Jamie.

Mrs. Swenson called, "Just a minute, please. I've got to have a word with Mr. Jackson."

"Certainly, dear," said the cheerful voice. "But don't take too long. We have a schedule to keep."

Barkley was moving again. When the chair stopped this time, he was determined to make a break for it.

He poked his way out of the blanket and started to leap from the chair. But Jamie fell on top of Barkley and a gray-haired man quickly spread a newspaper over them both. Strange hands pulled the dog onto the boniest pair of legs ever and held him there. Jamie slid out from under the paper, and the chair carrying Barkley zoomed off again.

"Come on, doggie," growled Mr. Jackson. "We're busting out of here."

Barkley heard a door slide open. He felt air ruffle the newspaper. The chair whirred along, then began to bump over uneven ground. At last they stopped and the newspaper came off. They were in a flower garden.

Jamie and the old man looked down at

Barkley and grinned.

"We did it!" the old man said proudly.

"Yes!" said Jamie, his thumb in the air. "Thanks a lot." He grabbed Barkley's leash and the dog jumped down.

"Glad to help," said Mr. Jackson. "I felt like one of those action heroes in a movie. Haven't had so much fun in years."

Jamie led Barkley around the outside of the building. They waited out front for his mom. On the way home, Jamie told his mother what had happened.

"That Mr. Peach is mean," he finished. "He just doesn't seem to understand the people at Sunny Acres."

"Now, Jamie," said his mother. "I'm sure Mr. Peach knows his business. It's not your problem."

Jamie made a face. "Well, can I at least go see Mrs. Williams again on Friday? The teachers have a meeting so we don't have school."

"Oh, dear," said Mrs. Boggs. "I forgot about

Friday. I have to be at work. I'll have to find a sitter. Maybe she can take you to Sunny Acres."

"A sitter?" Jamie objected. "What if I spend the day at Melissa's instead?"

His mother smiled and looked hopeful. "It's fine with me if it's all right with Melissa's mom."

*   *   *   *   *

After supper, the telephone rang. It was Mrs. Williams.

"Jamie," said Mrs. Williams. "I told my friend Mrs. Swenson about the bird you saw. She thinks it might be a cockatiel."

"A cockatiel?" Jamie repeated. "Is that something like a cuckoo?"

Mrs. Williams laughed. "No," she said. "It's more like a parakeet, only bigger. Most of them live in Australia."

"Gosh," said Jamie. "I wonder what's he's doing around here."

"Mrs. Swenson says that he was probably

someone's pet that escaped," said Mrs. Williams. "But the weather is getting colder now. If he stays outside, he'll get sick and die. Do you think you could catch him?"

"I'll try," Jamie promised.

"Good for you," she said. "But be gentle about it. Birds are more delicate than dogs."

"Right," said Jamie. "By the way, what did Mr. Peach want when he called you into his office?"

She grunted. "That man! He said Miss Case and I were troublemakers and we had better watch our steps. It sounded like a threat."

"What a creep," Jamie said.

"I agree. In fact, everyone I've talked to is hopping mad about the way you and Barkley were treated. I'm organizing a strike to demand that dogs be allowed to visit."

"What's a strike?" asked Jamie.

"Well, usually a strike happens because workers think that their company is being unfair in some way, so they refuse to work. At Sunny

Acres, we're refusing to play any more of their silly games—like bingo—until Mr. Peach gives in."

"Good for you," said Jamie. "I hope you win."

Mrs. Williams sighed. "Me, too. But Mr. Peach is pretty stubborn."

"Hmmm," said Jamie. "Maybe I could find a way to help."

"No, no, don't you worry about it," said Mrs. Williams. "Oops, I must go! I'm due at Mrs. Swenson's bird watchers' meeting. 'Bye."

*   *   *   *   *

The next day Melissa came over after school to help Jamie look for the cockatiel. Barkley helped, too. They checked every small hole in the house and the garage, but they didn't see the bird. They wandered to the backyard.

"Too bad," said Melissa, with a little shiver. "It's getting colder all the time. I hope that cockatiel doesn't get too cold and die."

"Yeah," Jamie agreed. "We've got to find him."

After Melissa left, Jamie called Mrs. Williams to report on his search.

"I know you did your best. Just keep trying," Mrs. Williams said in a worried tone. "Mrs. Swenson says cockatiels like fruit. Take some pieces of apple or orange with you next time."

"Okay," said Jamie. "So, how's your strike going?"

"Not good," she replied. "Mr. Peach says he doesn't care if we take part in the activities or not. In fact, he seems to prefer that we don't. We're getting discouraged."

"Don't give up," said Jamie. "I have an idea about how I can help you."

"Oh, please don't feel you need to get involved. We can handle this ourselves," she said. "But I do miss seeing Barkley."

"You're going to see him again," Jamie promised. "We'll find a way no matter what."

45

Barkley, who was listening from the corner, put his chin on his front paws and sighed.

Six

On Wednesday morning Barkley needed to go out early. Jamie opened the back door for the dog and went back inside. After Barkley took care of his business, he went to the bird feeder.

The cockatiel was eating there, hunched down behind a side rail. A stiff breeze blew its feathers. The bird shivered.

"Ruff," Barkley barked softly, his nose in the air.

The bird stopped eating and waddled to the edge of the feeder. It flew down and perched on a bush not far from Barkley.

Barkley made whining noises. He inched forward.

The bird paced back and forth on its branch, but did not fly away. Barkley moved closer. The bird cocked its head toward Barkley.

Suddenly a door slammed. Next Barkley heard the sound of running feet. The bird exploded into action and flew to the roof of the house.

Jamie ran around the side of the house. "Barkley, did you see it? The cockatiel was here again," he gasped.

The bird zipped behind the chimney, and Jamie looked around uncertainly. "But where did it go?" he asked.

Mrs. Boggs stuck her head out the door. "Jamie, please put Barkley in his kennel," she called. "It's time for your bus."

"But, Mom, you have to see this bird," the boy protested.

"Later, Jamie," said Mr. Boggs, appearing with Mrs. Boggs in the doorway. "The bus is coming."

"Okay, okay," said Jamie. "Come on, Barkley."

Jamie put Barkley in his pen and left. Soon after, Jamie got on his bus. Then Mr. and Mrs. Boggs drove away in their cars. Barkley sighed and lay down for another long wait.

Then he heard a familiar whistle. Barkley looked up to see the cockatiel above him. The dog did his best to imitate the bird's whistle. The bird responded with a noise that sounded almost like the sound Barkley had made.

Soon the cockatiel was inching his way down the side of the kennel, using his beak and his toes. This time Barkley stood his ground while the bird came lower and lower.

The cockatiel hopped down a few feet from Barkley's nose and began to dip its beak in and out of Barkley's dish. When Barkley eased forward, the bird turned his head and looked directly at the dog.

Just then a dark shadow covered them, and the bird froze. Barkley looked up to see a mass of feathers hurtling down at them.

Without thinking, Barkley shut his eyes and

leaped up and over the cockatiel. His teeth met the solid flesh of a bigger bird, but he couldn't hold onto the thing. When he opened his eyes, he saw a hawk soaring away over the garage. Barkley was left with a mouthful of feathers.

With his heart beating wildly, Barkley spit out the feathers and shuddered. Next to him, the cockatiel, too, was shaking.

Barkley nudged the bird gently with his nose. It snuggled up to Barkley and began to work through Barkley's fur with its beak. Finally the bird stepped away from the dog. With a quick whistle, it flew off.

Barkley wished he could get out of the pen as easily as that bird did, but he was glad he didn't need to worry about enemies diving at him from above.

* * * * *

When Jamie came home from school, he and Barkley looked for the cockatiel again.

Jamie's dad even helped, but again they failed to find the mysterious bird.

After supper, Jamie brushed Barkley. Then they got into the car. Barkley pressed his nose against the back window and watched the countryside roll by. He loved to ride in the car, but he didn't like to think about where they might be going.

When they stopped in front of a big metal building, Barkley groaned. They had arrived at their weekly 4-H dog class. Actually Barkley liked learning to follow Jamie's commands. It was the dog *class* he hated. He always seemed to get into trouble.

Kids and dogs were getting out of cars all around them. But Jamie had to drag Barkley out.

"Come on," Jamie urged. "You're doing great in dog class these days. Mrs. Redding isn't going to yell at you."

Barkley hoped Jamie was right.

Jamie's friend Melissa and her golden

retriever, Sadie, were just inside the door.

"Hi," she said. "We've been waiting for you. Did you find the cockatiel?"

Jamie shook his head. "No, not yet," he answered.

"Well, what's the latest on Mrs. Williams's strike?" she went on.

"Not good," said Jamie.

They wandered over toward the bleachers at the side of the building and sat.

"What's wrong?" Melissa asked.

Jamie shook his head sadly. "Mr. Peach is ignoring them. But I have an idea that might help."

"Tell me," she urged.

"Well," said Jamie, "there's no school this Friday. We could all bring our dogs to the park across the street from Sunny Acres. We could have a rally to support Mrs. Williams and her friends."

"Yeah," said Melissa. "We could carry signs and everything."

"Good idea," said Jamie. "But do you think the other kids will go for it?"

"Sure. Just ask them."

Jamie scuffed his shoe in front of him. "Would you ask them for me?" he begged.

"Why?" asked Melissa.

"Well," Jamie said. "Because I'm new and all." Jamie scratched Barkley behind the ears. Barkley liked that a lot.

"It's a really good idea—and it's yours," said Melissa. "You should be the one to ask."

Just then a tall, very serious woman called, "All right, class! Let's get started. Form a circle."

It was Mrs. Redding.

And Barkley just knew she was going to yell at him.

Seven

Melissa stood up when she heard Mrs. Redding.

"That's my signal to go meet with the advanced class," she said. "Good luck."

About half of the kids and dogs stayed outside with Melissa and Sadie. The rest went inside with Jamie and Barkley.

The inside group formed a circle. Barkley was delighted to find himself next to a white poodle he had a crush on. The poodle's owner was Danielle Redding. She was the 4-H leader's daughter. The two of them always did everything perfectly.

Mrs. Redding cleared her throat. "Class, let's start with some heeling."

Jamie turned Barkley to the left and made sure the dog was sitting straight. Barkley's nose was even with Jamie's left knee.

"Forward!" ordered Mrs. Redding.

"Barkley, heel," said Jamie.

Barkley knew what to do. Both Jamie and Melissa had worked with him on it the entire fall. So when Jamie stepped forward, Barkley stayed right next to his boy's knee no matter how fast or slow he walked.

"Halt!" said Mrs. Redding.

The entire circle stopped, and Barkley popped back into a sitting position next to Jamie. They practiced some more and then moved on to do a few other drills.

Mrs. Redding stopped them and said, "You are all showing real improvement, but when I watched some of you at the Fall Festival Dog Show, I saw problems."

The kids looked at each other.

Mrs. Redding kept talking, but Barkley's attention was on the poodle. She was so cute.

"Too many of your dogs were distracted by things outside the ring," said Mrs. Redding. There was a murmur of agreement.

"We want to fix that," she continued. "So I've asked some helpers to come tonight and try to distract your dogs on purpose."

Barkley leaned toward the poodle and whined. The poodle put her nose in the air and sniffed.

Mrs. Redding nodded to four kids over by the bleachers. They came over and stood at the side of the circle next to Mrs. Redding. Each carried a grocery sack.

Barkley glanced at them, then turned back to the poodle.

"I'm going to have you do some more heeling," Mrs. Redding went on. "But this time, be prepared for anything. Forward!"

"Barkley, heel," said Jamie.

Oops, the poodle was moving forward. Barkley wanted to do things right, so he walked forward with his nose at Jamie's knee. They passed the kids with the grocery sacks, and Barkley watched

carefully.

The class continued to circle, and Barkley started to walk by the kids with the sacks again. Suddenly the visitors pulled yo-yos out of their sacks and began to flip them around.

Barkley thought they were throwing things at him, so he pulled back. Immediately he was bumped from behind by a big, slobbery collie.

He shot forward and rear-ended the poodle. She turned to snap at him, leaving Barkley very embarrassed.

"Halt!" yelled Mrs. Redding. "Get your dogs back where they belong, and we'll try it again."

Danielle scowled at Barkley. She took the poodle to the other side of the circle. Barkley sighed.

The rest of the class went well, and finally it was time for refreshments. Everyone raced toward the cookies and juice.

Jamie drank his juice in one gulp. Then he took Barkley to the water fountain and ran water in the empty glass. Barkley drank for a long time. At last Jamie took a deep breath and led Barkley over to where Mrs. Redding was sitting, sipping her juice.

"Mrs. Redding," he said. "Could I ask the rest of the kids about something?"

She glanced over at him. "Okay," she said. "Do you want to talk to me about it first?"

"Uh—I don't think so," he answered, feeling nervous. He wanted to talk about this once—and only once—to the kids who could help him.

Jamie stayed near Mrs. Redding when the kids from the advanced class came in for their juice and cookies. Barkley sensed that his boy was very nervous, so he licked Jamie's hand and stood close.

Mrs. Redding clapped her hands and everyone quieted down. "Jamie Boggs has something to tell you," she announced. "Jamie?"

He felt his face turning red. He cleared his throat and began, "Yes, yes, well, I . . .," he croaked.

Someone giggled.

"Well, I'm here to say I need your help," he said at last.

The other kids looked curious.

"My friend Mrs. Williams moved into Sunny

Acres on Sunday," Jamie explained. "She and Barkley are really good friends, so I took him to Sunny Acres after school on Monday."

"I remember hearing about how Barkley practically saved her life," Mrs. Redding said, smiling. "Do you remember that, kids?"

A low murmur arose from the room.

Jamie broke in. "But Mr. Peach, who's in charge there, said that dogs aren't allowed inside." Jamie was trembling now, so Barkley leaned harder against the boy's leg. "Mrs. Williams is so upset that she and her friends are having a strike to change Mr. Peach's mind," Jamie went on. "I think we should help them. Maybe plan a rally or something."

"Would we get to carry signs?" asked a girl with a boxer. The girl was wolfing down cookies as she spoke.

"Sure," said Jamie. "We could meet at the park on Friday and march around in front of Sunny Acres."

The boy with the cocker spaniel sat on the

bleachers and crossed his legs. "Sounds like a good idea," he said. "But I can't come. We're going to the zoo."

"Me neither," said Danielle Redding. "I have ballet."

"Who'll make the signs?" asked a girl with a Sheltie.

"We will," said Melissa, coming over to stand next to Jamie. "At my house on Thursday night."

"I can't come," said the girl with the boxer. "That's my karate night."

"I'll make a sign, but I don't want to carry it," said a girl with a dachshund. "We might get in trouble."

"Yeah, what if we get arrested?" asked the girl with the Sheltie.

Whenever Jamie opened his mouth to say something, someone interrupted. He bent down and hugged Barkley. It seemed as if everyone liked the idea, but none of the kids wanted to get involved.

Barkley felt sad all over again.

Eight

"Come on, you guys," said Melissa. "We won't get in trouble. This is a free country. Sadie and I will be there. How about the rest of you?"

The kids started talking, and then Mrs. Redding clapped her hands again for quiet.

"Everyone, listen up!" she yelled. "We won't get anywhere without a good plan, and I'm not sure that a rally is the best plan to help Mrs. Williams."

"What else can we do?" asked Melissa.

Mrs. Redding looked thoughtful. "Well, I'm sure the man who runs Sunny Acres is reasonable. We could each write him a letter saying how much our dogs mean to us."

"Good idea," said the boy with the cocker spaniel.

"We could quote those studies that say people who have dogs live longer. And send some articles about how dogs are great companions for older people," said Mrs. Redding.

"Yeah," said the girl with the dachshund. "And we can't get in trouble just writing letters."

Jamie stood up. "But Mr. Peach thinks he's running a hospital," he said. "He thinks dogs carry germs."

"Then our letters will just have to change his mind about that," said Mrs. Redding. "Class, please write your letters tonight and give them to Danielle at school. She and I will deliver them to Sunny Acres on our way to her ballet class on Friday."

Everyone started talking again and some kids headed out the door. Jamie just stood there for a moment, but Melissa gave him a nudge toward the door.

"Do you think those letters will change Mr. Peach's mind?" she asked.

Jamie shrugged. "It's worth a try. I'll call Mrs. Williams Friday night after Mr. Peach has gotten the letters to see if things have changed at Sunny Acres."

"What if they haven't?" Melissa asked.

Jamie frowned. "Then I'll call some of the kids and try to have a rally on Saturday. Mom might even be able to drive me then."

"I'll help you call," Melissa promised.

On the way home, Jamie told his mother about his idea and what Mrs. Redding had said.

"She's right," Mrs. Boggs replied. "Letters and petitions are the way things get done in this country."

"But, Mom," Jamie said. "I don't think they are going to do the job with Mr. Peach. He's really stubborn. In fact, he's kind of a creep."

"Jamie, just give him a chance," said Mrs.

Boggs. "Wait until the letters are delivered before you get too angry with him."

Jamie sighed. "Okay," he agreed. "But Barkley and I are going to see Mrs. Williams again. I promised we would."

*   *   *   *   *

On Thursday morning, after Jamie left for school, Barkley lay near the front door of his kennel watching that weird bird. First the bird flew down to Barkley's water dish again. Then it poked its head inside Barkley's house. Then it flew out again, with something red in its mouth.

Barkley decided it was time to investigate. He got up and peeked inside his house.

His red rug was half gone!

"Ruff! Ruff!" barked Barkley. He wanted the bird to leave his rug alone.

The bird fluttered up, with the string in its beak, into the little oak tree on the other side of the kennel. A mass of red thread hung below it like an upside-down parachute.

The bird perched high in the tree. The mass of string caught in one of the lower branches and stayed there. The bird returned to Barkley.

This time it plopped down outside the door of the pen and looked through the wire. Barkley sniffed at the cockatiel. He felt like a prisoner.

The bird started walking up the outside of Barkley's cage. When it reached the lock on the door, it stopped to peck at the latch. Barkley yawned.

Suddenly the kennel door popped open, and the bird fluttered off. Barkley rose and looked out. He was free! He could go wherever he wanted.

The cockatiel flew toward the fence that led to the sheep pasture. Barkley started to follow. Then he remembered the German shepherd that lived over there. He did not plan to go into that pasture again.

But the bird flew beyond the fence and deeper into the pasture. Barkley wanted to avoid the German shepherd, but he also wanted to know where that bird was going.

Barkley looked quickly around to see if anyone was watching. Then he crawled under the fence and followed the bird. Sheep were scattered over the hills to the left, but the cockatiel headed to the right. Barkley ran after him.

The bird flew to a rotted gray tree stump that was about three times as tall as Jamie. Only a few branches remained on the tree and it was full of woodpecker holes. The cockatiel landed on a short branch, then ducked into one of the holes. Barkley watched the hole carefully. The bird stuck his head out again and whistled. Then it went back inside and stayed there.

Barkley wished he could tell the bird that this was a bad place for a home. The German shepherd and its owner could be dangerous.

But, of course, that was impossible.

So Barkley trotted back to his own yard and slipped under the fence. He lay down in the front yard and waited for Jamie.

Nine

Barkley heard the sound of a powerful motor.

It was the big, yellow bus that brought Jamie home every afternoon! Racing toward his boy, the dog barked and bounced and did his happy dance.

"Hey, who let you out?" Jamie asked. "I was sure that I hooked your door."

Barkley grinned and rolled over on his back.

Jamie walked around to the side of the house to look back at the kennel. "Gosh," he said, "where did all that stuff in the tree come from? I didn't know that tent caterpillars made red tents."

71

Barkley just flopped over on the ground and wiggled in the grass. It was fun seeing Jamie so confused.

"Oh, well," the boy said at last. "That's Dad's problem. Let's get our snacks and go look for that bird."

Barkley knew the word *bird*. Jamie had used it many times this week when he walked around the yard looking into every hole.

They went into the house. Jamie took a cookie for himself and threw Barkley a doggie treat. The boy took some bits of apple from the refrigerator, and they headed back outside.

"All right, bird, where are you?" Jamie said, looking around.

There was that word again—*bird*. Barkley knew what Jamie meant, and he knew where to find the bird. He galloped toward the fence at the edge of the sheep pasture.

Jamie followed, but he stopped when he saw where Barkley was going.

"Barkley, no!" the boy said firmly. "Sarge

lives back there. You don't want to fight with a German shepherd, do you?"

Barkley did remember. He remembered all too well. And while he did not want to fight with Sarge, he *knew* Jamie wanted the bird. Barkley was worried about the bird, too. So he slid under the fence and started into the pasture. Then he stopped and sat down facing Jamie.

"Ruff," barked the dog. "Ruff. Ruff."

"Barkley, come," Jamie demanded.

He was using the voice he used in dog training class. Barkley wanted to obey, but he also wanted Jamie to find the bird.

Barkley got up and trotted farther into the sheep pasture. He whined for Jamie to follow.

Jamie came closer to the fence. "Bad dog," he said. "Come back here! Bad dog."

Barkley cringed at the scolding, but moved slowly forward. He kept whining and hoping Jamie would understand.

Finally Jamie crawled under the fence and followed Barkley. The dog moved on toward the grove of trees where the bird was hiding.

Jamie was so angry now that he stomped his way forward. "Bad, bad, bad dog!" he shouted.

Barkley whined and moved on. He stopped at the old tree and sat in front of it. Jamie started running. When he got close to the stump, he tried to grab Barkley's collar.

The dog darted behind the tree. Jamie went after him and lunged at Barkley again. Barkley jumped away and returned to the front of the stump.

Then Barkley heard a low growl and saw a huge German shepherd slinking toward him. He froze and trembled. The hair at the back of the big dog's neck stood at attention. His teeth were bared. It was Sarge!

Jamie began to climb the old dead tree.

Sarge drew closer, his eyes fixed on Barkley.

Barkley swallowed hard. What should he do? If he ran, Sarge might get Jamie. If he stayed, the German shepherd would attack them both.

The big dog moved in closer, still growling.

Barkley backed up against the stump. He growled back. He was determined to fight for his boy.

Above Barkley, Jamie moved around to the front of the tree and looked up. He reached toward a new branch, then stared at the tree.

"Barkley," he said, gasping. "The cockatiel is right here."

Of course, Barkley already knew that. He had tried his best to show Jamie where the bird was hidden. But now he had bigger problems. He didn't dare take his eyes off Sarge. The German shepherd was obviously about to attack.

Then Barkley heard a flutter of wings, and the bird came out to land on the dog's head. It hissed at Sarge.

The German shepherd's eyes lit up and he growled louder. Barkley was too scared to breathe, but he knew one thing—he would fight to protect Jamie.

Suddenly the German shepherd leaped forward, his jaws open wide. Barkley braced himself, ready to bite back.

But Sarge never reached Barkley. Instead a screeching ball of feathers flew at Sarge's face.

"Help! Call the police!" cried the bird as it pecked the dog's nose. Sarge howled, backed up, and ran away. Barkley dared to breathe again.

The cockatiel flew to a nearby branch and shook itself violently. Barkley collapsed in a heap.

Jamie burst out laughing. "Wow!" said the boy as he started down the tree. "You're some bird! You even talk. Barkley, when did you guys get to be friends?"

Barkley looked up and grinned as Jamie hugged him.

"You knew that cockatiel was here, didn't you?"

Barkley grinned some more and wiggled. He sensed that Jamie was proud of him now.

"Good dog," said Jamie. "I'm sorry I didn't want to follow you at first." He patted Barkley. "You've found our bird, but how are we going to get him home?"

The boy fished in his pockets and brought out some bits of apple. He held them in the flat of his hand toward the bird.

"Nice bird," he said softly. "Have some goodies. Pretty bird. Come to my hand."

The bird looked at Jamie, first with one eye and then the other. "Pretty bird!" it declared.

Jamie grinned. "That's it. Pretty bird. Come on. Be a smart bird."

"Smart bird," the cockatiel agreed, and it began to whistle "Yankee Doodle."

"Wow, you *are* smart," Jamie said with a giggle. "Here, have some apple." But the bird stayed where it was.

Barkley whined, trying to tell the bird that Jamie was okay. But the bird ignored him.

Barkley wanted to get out of the sheep pasture before Sarge returned. So he got up and started toward Jamie's house. The cockatiel looked back at its hole in the dead tree, then at Barkley.

"Bye-bye," it said at last, and flew after Barkley.

"Nice going, Barkley," cried Jamie. He ran to catch up.

When they got to Jamie's yard, the bird landed in the little oak tree. Barkley stood below it. Jamie sat down next to Barkley. When the dog lay down and rolled on his back, Jamie scratched Barkley's belly. Barkley grunted happily.

Soon the bird flew to a branch closer to Barkley and Jamie. Jamie put a piece of apple on his head and leaned against the tree.

"Good bird. Come get a treat," said Jamie.

"Get a treat," the bird echoed.

The cockatiel eased himself down the tree trunk toward Jamie's head. Barkley watched and whined encouragement.

Finally the bird jumped onto Jamie's head,

grabbed a piece of apple, and flew away again.

"Yummy," the bird declared as it pecked at the apple on a branch above them.

"Smart bird," Jamie responded. "Come get another treat."

"Get a treat," said the bird.

This time it stayed on Jamie's head longer. Jamie put the next bit of apple on his shoulder. Again the bird took it.

The fourth time the bird returned, it sat on Jamie's shoulder. "Pretty bird," said the boy, holding out his finger.

"Smart bird," said the cockatiel. He hopped on his finger.

"Smart bird," Jamie agreed, and he closed his other hand around it. "Wait until I tell Mrs. Williams about this!"

Ten

Jamie's mom was surprised to see the cockatiel. "What a pretty bird," she said, studying it closely. "Where did you find it?"

"Pretty bird," the cockatiel agreed.

Mrs. Boggs grinned. "Oh, he's smart, too."

"Smart bird," the cockatiel echoed. "Get a treat."

Jamie pulled the bird close to him. That seemed to quiet it down. "He was hiding in a hollow tree. Barkley found him and got him to come to me."

"Smart dog, too," said Mrs. Boggs, smiling at Barkley.

"Can we keep the bird?" Jamie wanted to know.

Mrs. Boggs shook her head. "No, Barkley is the only pet we need. We'll run an ad in the paper and see if we can find the bird's owner."

"But what do we do with him now?" Jamie asked.

"I'll call your father and have him stop and get a bird cage on his way home," she said.

She went to the phone, called Jamie's father, and spoke briefly. Then she returned to report, "Dad said he'll be home soon with the cage."

"'Soon' with Dad could mean *hours*," Jamie complained. "Do I have to hold this bird until then?"

"No, I don't think so," said Mrs. Boggs. "We could put him in the guest bathroom."

Barkley was beginning to feel left out, so he pushed against Jamie's leg. Jamie patted the dog.

"Yes, we know," said the boy. "You're a hero. You found the bird. Now he'll stay warm and not get sick."

All three of them took the bird to the guest

bathroom. After they were all in, Mrs. Boggs shut the door.

Jamie was about to let the cockatiel go, when his mom shouted, "Wait! Let me put away some of this." She grabbed some towels and put them into the linen cupboard. "I've heard birds can be messy."

"Okay now?" Jamie asked.

"Okay," she agreed.

Jamie opened his hand and the cockatiel zoomed straight toward the window. "Oh, no," cried Jamie. "Look out for the glass!" He lunged toward the window and waved the bird away.

The bird careened down toward the toilet.

"Yipes!" yelped Mrs. Boggs, tripping over Jamie. "Not in there." She quickly closed the lid.

The bird swooped on toward the toilet paper and caught some in his feet.

"Ruff," barked Barkley, nudging the cockatiel away.

A piece of toilet paper sailed after the bird as

it flew up to the shower bar.

"Hey, take it easy," cried Jamie, staggering against a wall.

"Yes, calm down, you crazy bird," Mrs. Boggs said, gasping.

The cockatiel perched on the shower bar and screeched, "Help! Call the police."

"Aha!" said Jamie. "Now I know how that red stringy mess got up in the tree." He explained about the strange collection of red string that he had seen in the tree earlier.

The bird actually seemed to listen to Jamie's story for a while. Then it began pecking at one of the rings on the shower curtain rod.

"Do we dare leave him here alone?" Mrs. Boggs asked. The bird moved up and down the shower curtain rod pecking at the rings.

"I don't know," said Jamie. He slid down to sit on the floor. "He gets pretty wild."

Barkley came over and nudged Jamie's hand. He wanted Jamie to pet him, and Jamie did.

"Barkley," the boy said. "I used to think you were good at getting into trouble. But this bird is something else."

"Pretty bird. Get a treat," said the bird.

Jamie searched his pockets, then shook his head.

"No more treats," he told the bird.

"Get a treat," the cockatiel demanded. It opened its beak and fluffed its feathers.

"I hope your father gets here soon," said Mrs. Boggs. "The bird is getting restless again."

Barkley heard the sound of a car. He ran to the door of the bathroom, tail wagging.

"Hello! I'm home," called Mr. Boggs. "Where is everyone?"

Mrs. Boggs got up and went to the door. "We're in the bathroom," she called. Barkley backed out of her way.

"What are you doing in there?" asked Mr. Boggs.

Then the door swung open, right in Mrs. Boggs's face! She staggered back into Barkley,

and he jumped back farther. Jamie, who was just getting to his feet, tripped over Barkley and fell backward into the bathtub.

The bird screeched and feathers flew. It let go of the shower curtain rod and landed on Jamie's head.

"Help!" screeched the cockatiel. "Call the police!"

Mr. Boggs pushed his way in saying, "What on earth?"

Next, the bird swooped in the direction of the open door. Mr. Boggs slammed the door just in time. The cockatiel circled the room, then perched on the sink and looked at itself in the mirror.

"Pretty bird," it told its reflection. Then it soared back up to the shower curtain rod and shook itself again.

Barkley's ears hurt and his body felt sore. He huddled back behind the toilet, trying not to get stepped on.

"Did you bring the cage?" asked Mrs. Boggs.

"Yes, it's in the kitchen," said Mr. Boggs. "Should I go get it?"

"I'm not sure we dare open the door," Mrs. Boggs answered.

"I can do it," said Jamie. "I'm smaller so I can sneak through if you just open it a crack. I'll get some fruit, too, to help us catch the bird."

"Okay," said Mrs. Boggs. "Your father and I will try to keep the bird away from the door while you slip out."

Jamie eased himself out of the bathtub and crawled around his mother. His father leaned against one wall to let Jamie by. Barkley slid after Jamie and Mr. and Mrs. Boggs closed the door behind them.

Barkley was happy to be out of the bathroom. Things were too crazy in there.

Just then the phone rang. Jamie ran to answer it. It was Melissa.

"Oh, hi," said Jamie. "Guess what? I caught the bird and it's in the bathroom."

"Great," she replied. "Have you told Mrs. Williams?"

"Not yet," said Jamie. "and I can't talk long. The cockatiel is tearing up the bathroom, and my parents are in there with him. I've got to go rescue them."

"Wow," said Melissa. "I hope you have better luck with that bird than we did with those letters."

"What happened?" asked Jamie.

"I just talked to Danielle. She and her mom took the letters to Sunny Acres, but Mr. Peach barely looked at them. Then he told his secretary to deal with them."

Jamie groaned. "It doesn't sound good. We may still have to have our rally."

"That's what I think," she agreed.

"Jamie!" called a muffled voice from the bathroom. "Hurry up."

"Oops," said Jamie. "Sorry, Melissa. I've got to go. I'll call you later."

Then he hung up, dashed to the refrigerator,

and took out some raisins. Grabbing the cage, he raced back to the bathroom. Barkley followed.

It was time to catch that bird.

Eleven

When Jamie slipped into the bathroom this time, he told Barkley to wait outside. "It's too crowded in there," he explained. "I can catch the cockatiel by myself with these raisins."

Jamie closed the door, and Barkley heard Mr. Boggs say, "Come on, bird, get in the cage." Then he heard some bumping and "Ouch! He nipped me!" Then all was quiet again.

"Pretty bird," said Jamie. "Come, get a treat."

There was silence.

"The poor thing is afraid with so many of us around," Mrs. Boggs said at last. "Dad, you and I need to leave and let Jamie and Barkley handle this."

"Yes," Mr. Boggs agreed. "But move slowly and quietly. We don't want to scare him again."

Barkley heard movement. Then the door opened and Mr. and Mrs. Boggs came out slowly.

"Go help, Jamie," Mr. Boggs told Barkley, pushing him into the bathroom.

Barkley put on his brakes. He'd had enough of the bird's swooping and screeching. But Mr. Boggs was strong, and the dog found himself back in the bathroom.

Jamie reached down to pat Barkley. "Good dog," he said. "Talk to that bird, will you? Tell him he'll be safer in this cage."

Barkley wasn't sure what Jamie wanted, but he could see that the bird was frightened. So Barkley inched forward, making his high-pitched whines.

"Pretty bird," said Jamie. "Come, get a treat."

The bird cocked its head to look at Barkley. Then it studied Jamie and the raisins in his outstretched hand. Barkley and Jamie didn't move.

At last the cockatiel hopped down onto Barkley's head and stretched its neck toward Jamie. Jamie eased the raisins forward. The bird took one. Jamie offered his finger and the bird stepped on.

"Whew!" said Jamie, closing his hand over the cockatiel. "I'm glad that's over." He put the bird inside the cage and shut the door.

After picking up the cage, Jamie opened the bathroom door and stepped out. "Ta-dah!" he said, holding the cage up high. "Barkley did it again."

"Good dog," said Mr. Boggs.

"Yes, good for you, Barkley," added Mrs. Boggs.

With the bird safely in the cage, Mrs. Boggs made a quick supper and the family sat down to eat. At first they talked about the bird and finding its owner. Then Jamie remembered that they had another more serious problem on their hands. "Mrs. Redding delivered our letters to Mr. Peach today."

"Wonderful," said Mrs. Boggs. "What did Mr. Peach have to say about them?"

"Nothing," Jamie said. "He barely looked at them. Then he told his secretary to deal with them."

"Hmm," said Mr. Boggs. "Sounds as if this guy is a regular dictator."

"Yes, he's being unreasonable," Mrs. Boggs agreed. "What do you and Mrs. Williams plan to do about it?"

"I'll call her right after supper," Jamie promised. "Mom, if we decide to have a rally on Saturday, will you drive me?"

She thought a moment. "Yes, I will," she said. "Maybe Mr. Peach will pay attention when he sees that you kids are serious about this."

"Great!" said Jamie. "I'm finished eating. May I call Mrs. Williams now?"

Both parents nodded.

A few minutes later Jamie was telling Mrs. Williams about how he and Barkley caught the cockatiel.

"Hooray!" she cheered. "Barkley's a hero again. Wait until I tell Mrs. Swenson."

"Now we have to try to find the bird's owner," said Jamie.

"Yes, I suppose so," said Mrs. Williams. "But I'd like to see the cockatiel before you do."

"Not much chance of that," said Jamie. "Mr. Peach would have a fit if we brought in a bird."

"He'd go bonkers," she agreed. "He still thinks this is a hospital or something."

"My 4-H club wrote letters asking him to let dogs visit," said Jamie. "But I guess they didn't help."

"Nope," said Mrs. Williams, "and our strike was a failure, too. There's nothing else we can do."

"Oh, yes, there is," said Jamie. "Some of us kids and our dogs are going to have a rally in front of Sunny Acres on Saturday morning. We'll carry signs and see if we can get Mr. Peach's attention."

"Really?" said Mrs. Williams. "You kids

would do that for us? Why, that's wonderful. In fact, maybe we'll stage a demonstration of our own on Saturday. I'm sure Miss Case will help us."

"All right!" said Jamie. "See you then."

*   *   *   *   *

Jamie and Barkley spent Friday at Melissa's house, calling the other 4-H members and making signs for Saturday. They got pretty discouraged. Most of the kids thought Jamie's idea was a good one, but they all seemed too busy to help.

The signs turned out great, though. Jamie's read: "DOGS ARE GOOD MEDICINE! LET THEM COME TO VISIT!"

Melissa's sign read: "DOGS ARE SENIOR CITIZENS' BEST FRIENDS, TOO."

Jamie and Melissa talked for a while about how great it would be to have pets at Sunny Acres. The more they talked, the more excited they became about the rally.

But when Saturday morning came, Jamie didn't feel as hopeful about the rally.

"What's the matter, Jamie?" asked Mr. Boggs. "Aren't you excited about the rally?"

"Not really," said Jamie. "I'm afraid no one will come but Melissa and me and our dogs."

Mr. Boggs reached behind the couch and pulled out a piece of cardboard. It read: "MAKE OUR NURSING HOMES HOMEY: ALLOW DOGS."

Jamie looked puzzled. "Whose sign is that?"

"Mine," said Mr. Boggs with a grin. "I'm coming with you."

"Me, too," said Mrs. Boggs, appearing from the kitchen with her own sign. It read: "DOGS GIVE LOVE! LET THEM IN."

Then Jamie smiled and said, "Thanks, guys. Come on, Barkley. It's time to go."

Mrs. Boggs reached for the cockatiel's cage. "The bird should come, too," she said. "Dogs aren't the only pets that should visit Sunny Acres."

"Good idea," said Mr. Boggs. "If we win to-day, we can use the bird to point that out."

Jamie's dad drove over and picked up Melissa. Then they headed to Sunny Acres and parked in front of a small park across the street. Since no one else was around, they didn't get out of their cars right away. No other cars were there yet.

"Well," Jamie said with a sigh. "I guess we really are the only ones coming."

"It's still early," Mrs. Boggs pointed out.

Melissa nodded. "Meagan and Joni sounded like they *might* come."

Barkley pressed his nose against the window. Then he barked once to get Jamie's attention. A police car was pulling up behind them. A police officer got out.

Mr. Boggs rolled down his window. "Is there a problem, officer?"

The police officer looked in at them. "Not yet," he said. "But we got a call from a Mr. Peach. He said some wild kids were coming here to stage a protest march. Do you know anything about that?"

Mr. Boggs shrugged. "Do these kids and their dogs look wild?"

The police officer laughed. "No, I guess not." He went back to his car and got in. Then he made a U-turn in front of them, parked at the entrance to Sunny Acres, and went inside.

"How on earth did Mr. Peach find out about this?" Mr. Boggs wondered. "He must spy on the residents."

"Yeah," said Mrs. Boggs. "But why did he call the police?"

"Gosh," said Jamie. "Now I sort of hope no one *will* show up."

"Forget that idea," said Melissa. "Here come Meagan and Joni and their dogs."

Barkley knew the dogs from class. He put his nose to the glass and barked at the dogs.

The two girls went to Mrs. Boggs's window. "Did you see that police officer?" asked the girl with the dachshund. "I told you we were going to get in trouble."

"No, we won't," Mrs. Boggs assured her. "We're not doing anything wrong. And we're on a public street in front of a public park."

A van pulled in behind them. Three kids got out with their dogs. One of them was the poodle that Barkley liked so much.

"It's Danielle Redding," said Jamie. "I didn't think she'd come."

"Mrs. Redding is driving the van!" Melissa said. "She's getting out, and she has a sign, too."

Then another car and another van arrived. More kids and dogs got out. They all carried signs. Barkley got more and more excited. He wanted to get out and see the other dogs.

Finally Melissa said, "Let's go." She opened the door and stepped out with Sadie. Barkley pulled Jamie out the door after her.

It was time for the rally to begin.

Twelve

"Well, we're here," said the boy with the cocker spaniel. "Now what do we do?"

"Jamie, you started this," said the girl with the collie. "What's the plan?"

"I . . . I . . .," Jamie muttered, confused. He leaned back against the side of the van.

"Ruff, ruff," barked Barkley. Barkley knew Mrs. Williams was across the street in that building, and he wanted to see her. He pulled Jamie around to the front of the van, and he sat on the curb so he could look across to Sunny Acres.

"Hey, Barkley has a good idea," said Melissa. "Let's hold up our signs and face Sunny

Acres and have our dogs sit beside each of us."

The dozen or so kids with their dogs and the adults, including Mrs. Redding, hurried to follow her directions.

"What now?" asked the girl with the poodle.

"Ruff! Ruff! Ruff!" barked Barkley. He wanted to tell Mrs. Williams he was here.

"Right, Barkley," said a girl with a boxer. "Let's let Sunny Acres know we're here."

The girl with the Sheltie started to howl like a dog. Then all the dogs did, too. They made a terrible racket.

About that time, the side door of Sunny Acres opened. A procession of people walked or rolled down the sidewalk toward the front of the building. Barkley saw Mrs. Williams, so he barked even louder and strained at his leash.

Then the front door opened. Mr. Peach and the police officer came down the steps. They seemed to be arguing.

As he reached the curb, Mr. Peach stepped away from the police officer and glared at him.

Next Mr. Peach glared at the kids and their dogs. Gradually everyone got quiet and stared back.

"Go away!" yelled Mr. Peach. "You can't make all this noise outside my hospital. I'll have this officer arrest you." The police officer said something to Mr. Peach and shook his head.

"This isn't a hospital!" shouted Mrs. Swenson, wheeling her chair toward Mr. Peach. "It's our home."

"We pay good money to live here," said Mr. Jackson, the man who had hidden Barkley and had carried him around in his wheelchair. "We have our rights."

"And we love dogs—and other animals," said Mrs. Williams. She raised her arm in the air. "Bring back Barkley! Bring back Barkley!"

"Bring back Barkley!" said Mrs. Swenson.

"BRING BACK BARKLEY!" the crowd roared.

Barkley ducked his head. He liked to get

attention, but this was ridiculous.

Mr. Peach talked quietly to the police officer and pointed toward Barkley. The police officer shrugged and started across the street. The crowd grew quiet. Barkley sensed his humans were nervous and so was he.

"Who started this?" asked the police officer as he neared them. He looked up and down the line of kids and dogs. "Who's in charge?"

"*He* is," said the girl with the dachshund, pointing at Jamie. "This was all his idea."

Jamie crouched down and hugged Barkley.

"But we wanted to help him," said Melissa. She and Sadie moved closer to Jamie and Barkley.

"We're not breaking any laws," Mr. Boggs pointed out. "You can tell Mr. Peach I've already called the newspaper. I wonder what the town will think when they read about how he treats the people who live at Sunny Acres."

The police officer looked over at Mr. Boggs. "You did?" he asked, stroking his chin. "Yes, I think I will have another little talk with Mr. Peach."

The police officer turned and walked back to Mr. Peach. They talked quietly some more. Then Mr. Peach waved his hands and shook his fist, but the police officer shook his finger at Mr. Peach.

Finally Mr. Peach paused and stared into space. Then he motioned to Barkley and his supporters that they should come over to Sunny Acres' side of the street.

When Jamie stood up, Barkley surged forward, straining at his leash. The people with Barkley followed. Mrs. Williams and her friends moved toward Mr. Peach, too.

Mr. Peach looked grim. "Ahem," he began. "Officer Peters has informed me that you people have a right to demonstrate."

The crowd nudged each other and nodded.

"And I don't want any bad publicity, especially since I just took over at Sunny Acres. So . . ."

The crowd leaned forward expectantly, so Barkley did, too.

Mr. Peach made a face as if the words to come were going to hurt. "I've decided to let dogs visit Sunny Acres."

"HOORAY!" cried the crowd. Barkley and the other dogs barked to help celebrate.

"How about birds?" asked Mrs. Boggs, and she brought out the cage she had been carrying behind her back.

Mr. Peach's eyes flashed and he opened his mouth to say something, but the people in the crowd crossed their arms and stared at him. Finally Mr. Peach swallowed hard and forced a smile.

"Okay," he said, "bring on the birds, the cats, the pet monkeys. I know when I'm licked."

"Hooray!" said Mrs. Swenson.

"HOORAY!" the whole crowd yelled.

About that time, a van pulled up. A lady with a notebook and a man with a big camera got out and started talking to people.

Mr. Peach eyed them, then put on his warmest smile. "Everyone please come inside," he said sweetly. "Miss Case, would you arrange for some refreshments?"

"Certainly," she said with a grin and headed in the front door.

The police officer got in his car and drove away. Barkley and his family made their way across the street to Mrs. Williams and Mrs. Swenson.

As soon as Barkley got close to Mrs. Williams, he couldn't help himself. He took a flying leap and landed right on Mrs. Williams's lap.

"Oh, Barkley, Love," cried Mrs. Williams, hugging the dog. "You were so clever. I saw how you led the demonstration." Barkley yipped twice and wagged his tail. Then he covered Mrs. Williams's face with wet kisses.

"May I see the cockatiel?" asked Mrs. Swenson.

Mrs. Boggs held the bird's cage at Mrs. Swenson's eye level.

"Oh, he's a beauty," said Mrs. Swenson.

"Pretty bird!" the cockatiel declared, and everyone chuckled.

"Smart bird, too," said Jamie.

"Smart bird," the cockatiel said.

"Oh, how wonderful—a talking bird," said Mrs. Swenson. "I'm going to work on Mr. Peach. If you don't find this bird's owners, I want Sunny Acres to adopt him. What do you think?"

"Good idea," said Jamie.

"Smart," the cockatiel said.

"Ruff, Ruff," Barkley barked. He thought it was a good idea, too. Then he would have the Boggs's house all to himself again!

He snuggled deeper into Mrs. Williams's arms. And he had Mrs. Williams back, too. He couldn't wait to visit her and all of the other nice people at Sunny Acres.

Barkley was back!

About the Author

MARILYN D. ANDERSON grew up on a dairy farm in Minnesota. Her love for animals and her twenty-five years of training and showing horses are reflected in many of her books.

A former music teacher, Marilyn taught band and choir for seventeen years. She specialized in percussion and violin. These days, she stays busy training young horses, riding in dressage shows, working at a library, giving piano lessons, and, of course, writing books. Marilyn and her husband live in Bedford, Indiana.

Mrs. Anderson's other books include *Come Home, Barkley; Nobody Wants Barkley;* and *No Home for Shannon.*